AUTOBIOGRAPHY OF A VILLAIN

AUTOBIOGRAPHY OF A VILLAIN

CHINDU SREEDHARAN

EPIC RETOLD

First published in the United Kingdom in 2019

Copyright © 2019 Chindu Sreedharan

Print: 978-1-78972-799-9
ASIN: B0821WVFC7

www.epicretold.co.uk

Cover: Arijit Ganguly

To the brothers I lost: Balu, Vinod, Siby

AUTHOR'S NOTE

FOR MOST FOLKS familiar with Indian mythology, Duryo-
dhana is the epitome of villainy. He is the Shylock, the Long
John Silver, the Bill Sykes, the Professor Moriarty, the Lord
Voldemort, the Night King of the Mahabharata.

Vyasa, the original scribe of the great Indian epic, writes
of ill omens all over Hastinapur when Duryodhana was
born. Later, on more than one occasion, he is described as
the son born to destroy the Kaurava clan by characters as
venerable as Vidura.

Duryodhana's own actions—the way those are usually
depicted, that is—give no doubt he is cut from a particularly
dark cloth. Where his cousins, the Pandavas led by Yudhistira, are pristine in their words and deeds (bar occasional
aberrations such as polyandry, gambling, and wife-pawn-
ing), Duryodhana is shown as jealous, greedy, petty.

Yet there is much good, much magnanimity, in him. One
need only look at the way Duryodhana stood up for Karna,
'the son of the charioteer', during their coming-of-age skills
demonstration to see that. How many young princes would

have the courage to tell their elders that their stance of barring someone from a competition based on birth is just plain wrong? One could argue that Duryodhana was motivated by his dislike of the Pandavas in that action, but it could also be seen as indicative of his outlook on equality, non-discrimination, and human rights.

I became fascinated with Duryodhana's character when I was halfway through writing *Epic Retold* (Harper Collins India), narrating the Mahabharata from Bhima's perspective. One cannot tell the story of Bhima without speaking of Duryodhana. And the more I thought about his character, the more I began to like him. My respect for Duryodhana grew further when I considered his duel with Bhima on the sidelines of the Kurukshetra battlefield.

Yudhistira—silly Yudhistira!—gives away all the advantage his brothers have gained over eighteen days of war when he challenges Duryodhana to a duel and grandly announces that Duryodhana can pick any weapon, and any Pandava to fight—and if he won, the kingdom would be his.

What does Duryodhana do? He does the honourable thing. He picks the strongest Pandava, his arch-enemy, Bhima. Not Yudhistira, or Arjuna, or Nakula, or Sahadeva— any of whom he could have broken like a twig.

So that is the Duryodhana of this novella. He doesn't always take the easiest path, or do the 'correct' thing. Instead, he does the 'right' thing. He has a morality of his own, and he is not afraid to stand up for his beliefs. This Duryodhana is no superhero. He is human, flawed, like most of us—but with a lot of good in him.

It is challenging to try and capture all that complexity, all those nuances, in a short rendition such as this, across 18 episodes. Besides recasting Duryodhana, I have attempted to see if the world's longest epic can be condensed into, well, a rather long short story.

I hope I have done some justice to all that. I hope you like my Duryodhana.

Chindu Sreedharan

PROLOGUE

I wake to the last afternoon of my life not knowing whether I want to live but certain I will die before nightfall.

Eighteen days. Yet the killing is not done.

How piteous our final stand! How we crumbled! We had not even lasted half a day! By now they would be scouring the battlefield, tending to their wounded, silencing our dying, turning over corpses looking for me.

Or had they already assembled the trackers, sent out the search parties?

Not that it matters. The sun still has strength and the trail I left behind, it is a sight for even blind men.

They will be here. Soon.

I sit up slowly, swallowing the tide of pain that washes over me. The wet ground squelches when I reach to lean against a tree-stump, half-rotten and harmless but jutting from the river mud like the yawning mouth of a vengeful alligator.

For the first time since I entered the swamp, I feel the

mud. It is cold, soothing against the cuts on my back, and I scoop up fistfuls to cover my chest and neck.

I sit still, staring through the clump of trees that strains to filter the afternoon sun. Beyond lies the lake. Dvaipayana, the foresters call it. And beyond it snakes the silver of the Hiranvati river.

I see smoke rising from the crematorium on its green banks, rising above the woodlands, like giant bats hunting in daylight.

Souls bound for heaven. Or hell. Who can tell?

Up the river, towards the east, is the battleground. Kurukshetra. That's the way they will come. Along the riverside, all the way till where it meets the lake, then across the woods, to this watery isle.

And then? How will it end?

I try not to think. I am not fond of living, but neither do I crave death. Strange, this indifference that has crept up on me. Is this how death begins?

I close my eyes and wait for my killers.

I wait, for my brothers.

1

The maid who came to get us from the elephant stalls was breathing hard, as if she had run all the way from the palace. Beads of sweat trembled on her brow.

'Come, my princes,' she said, with a hurried curtsy. 'The queen wants you.'

Dushasana, who was handing me palm fronds to feed my tusker, stopped and looked at me. Signalling my younger brother to continue, I moved closer to the elephant.

'We have only started,' I said. 'Tell mother we will come soon.'

We were not allowed in the elephant stalls by ourselves, but at this time of the morning, there was no one to stop us. The palace was barely awake, and the mahouts were all at the north entrance, overseeing the feed for the day being brought in.

'Not soon,' the maid said. 'Now!'

Taking Dushasana's hand, she pulled him to his feet and reached for me. I stumbled and almost fell backward trying to evade her.

'This is no time for games, prince,' the maid said, grabbing my shoulder. 'Listen to me!'

'Let go!' I said. 'You should not speak to me like that!'

'Yes, child. And you can have me whipped for it when you become king. But so long as you are five years of age, and my care, you will listen. Now, hurry along!'

The palace was astir by the time we arrived. Servants hurried along the hallway and corridors, and I saw at least half a dozen chariots ready at the main entrance.

Some friendly king must be visiting Hastinapur. I wondered who it was.

When we passed by the great hall, I spotted Grandfather Bhishma amidst a group of courtiers. Even though I could not see his face, I knew it was him. Nobody had his head of grey. Nobody stood like him, so tall and straight.

Grandfather Bhishma was not really our grandfather, but our grandfather's elder brother. Our real grandfather's name was Krishnadvaipayana. He was a sage who wandered the forests. I met him once, when I was small. I did not like him much.

On that occasion, Grandfather Krishnadvaipayana had lifted me on to his lap with arms so thin I was scared they would break. He smelled of sweat and sandalwood.

I had sat on his lap without protest, but when he leaned to hug me, his beard, yellow and matted, tickled and I had pulled away. Everyone had laughed, Grandfather Krishnadvaipayana the loudest.

When the laughter subsided, grandfather had asked, 'When you grow up, what kind of a warrior do you want to be?'

'A maharathi,' I said without hesitation. 'One who can singlehandedly defeat a thousand warriors. I want to be like Grandfather Bhishma!'

4

'Oh? Not like your father Dhritarashtra?'

I did not know why he asked that question. Everyone knew my father was born blind, so he never had the opportunity to be a great warrior.

'My father has the strength of a thousand rogue elephants,' I had said, squirming out of his grasp. 'I too will have that strength when I grow up. I will be unconquerable!'

As we drew closer, I saw Grandfather Bhishma was saying something to Uncle Vidura, our father's half-brother. Uncle nodded.

Noticing us, grandfather called out to the maid. 'Ah, Sugadha, you have found the children!' he said. 'Get them ready! They are already at the outer gates!'

Hurrying behind Sugadha into the south wing, I could not contain my curiosity.

'Who is coming? Is it the Gandharians? Is it Uncle Shakuni?'

Uncle Shakuni was my mother's younger brother. He visited often, always laden with gifts, always willing for a game of dice and clever magic tricks. Once he had made our younger sister Dusshala disappear—right in front of our eyes!

When the maid did not respond, I stopped, bringing us all to a halt. I am only five, but I am strong. Very strong.

The maid sighed and turned to me. 'No, prince, it is not your Uncle Shakuni. It is your Aunt Kunti and her sons!'

I was astounded. Uncle Pandu, my father's younger brother, had left Hastinapur years ago, embracing vanaprastha. His wives, our aunts Kunti and Madri, had gone with him. Nobody had told me they had children. Why were they coming back?

Sensing I would not get answers from Sugadha just yet, I allowed her to lead us to the bathing quarters. The wooden tubs there were already filled with steaming water and maids awaited with scented oils to wash us.

After the bath, as the servants hurriedly attired me in ceremonial garbs, I remembered Sugadha had said nothing about Uncle Pandu. Was he returning, too?

Then a more disturbing thought occurred to me. The maid had said Aunt Kunti had brought her sons.

'Are Aunt Kunti's sons older?' I asked.

'Only one,' Sugadha said. 'Yudhistira is your elder by one year. Bhima is your age, Arjuna one year younger. Nakula and Sahadeva are twins and younger still. Now sit quiet while I finish with your hair!'

I waited a moment before I asked, 'If Yudhistira is older, who is the crown prince now?'

Sugadha did not answer. But when she picked up the yuvaraja's crown studded with a single blood-red jewel and set it on my head, I felt her fingers pressed down harder than usual.

2

The woman who stood with bowed head before Father, white-clad, sobbing, must be Aunt Kunti. I noticed the top of her head barely reached Father's chest.

From the hushed conversations of courtiers and the whispers in the hallway, I had gathered the reason for her tears. Uncle Pandu was no more. And Madri, our uncle's younger wife, had ended her life on his pyre.

When Aunt Kunti looked up, I saw the tales the maids tell about her are true. She was beautiful. Aunt Madri was said to have been even more beautiful and the palace had mourned for months when she had left.

Sensing someone at my arm, I turned around. Dusshala. My little sister had squeezed herself between Dushasana and me.

'Brother, there!' she said. 'That boy looks just like you!'

I looked to where Grandfather Bhishma stood amidst sages. Next to him, I counted five boys. They wore no upper garments, no ornaments. No footwear either.

The biggest among them stood a little apart from his

siblings. This must be Aunt Kunti's eldest, Yudhistira. He was tall, taller than me perhaps. Big, built like one of those forest people.

He looked nothing like me.

'Doesn't he?' Dusshala asked.

'No,' I said. 'Now silence! I want to watch.'

The big boy was staring at Father. His eyes rested on Father's face for a long time, then on the fifty-four strand rakshmikalapam necklace on his chest. The boy took in the golden throne.

Next he glanced at the huge marble column near where we stood. Craning his neck, he studied the dome of the ceiling.

There was bewilderment on his face. Incredulity. As if he could not believe what he was seeing.

I would never have that look of incomprehension on my face.

Suddenly, perhaps sensing our presence, the boy looked in our direction. Surprise, which gave way to recognition. When he caught my eye, he stared obstinately, as if willing me to look away.

I did not.

Grandfather Bhishma bent and whispered something. One of the brothers detached himself from the group, walked forward, and climbed the twelve steps to the dais where my Father was seated.

Prostrating at Father's feet, he said in the correct manner, 'I, Yudhistira, son of King Pandu, bow before you, O King!'

Oh! This was Yudhistira? I took another look at my elder cousin.

He was shorter than me. Chubby. Soft shoulders, weak chest. Dushasana could best him easily, I was certain.

Yudhistira listened to Father gravely, looking respectful.

The big boy now approached the dais. I had expected him to be slow and clumsy, but he walked lightly. He was awkward when he prostrated, though, and his salutation was all but incoherent.

'So tall already!' Father said, embracing the boy. 'Bhima has grown bigger than Duryodhana! You will make a fine warrior!'

Bhima. So this is the second son. The one Sugadha had said was my age.

I watched a dark, whip-thin boy, taut as a drawn bowstring, approach Father. Arjuna, I heard. Grandfather Bhishma himself brought up the two younger children, who were bawling.

Father rose when the salutations were over and a hush descended over the hall. Sanjaya, my Father's aide who acted as his eyes, quickly moved to his side.

'I mourn my brother, but I am glad for the gift of his family,' Father said. 'I have five more sons now. Hastinapur is blessed!'

As Father made his exit holding Sanjaya's hand, I saw the big boy staring at me again.

Turning on my heel, I followed Father.

3

_____

'W hy?'

Mother's voice was quiet. But behind her blindfold, I sensed fire.

'I-I did not start it,' I said.

'Look at me.'

Mother sat straight and still, black cloth wound tight around her pale face. Everyone knew the story of that blindfold: how my mother had vowed to cover her eyes and never see again when she agreed to marry my father, who was blind.

I had never been able to hold her gaze—not even through that blindfold. What colour are her eyes? Pale, like Uncle Shakuni's? The Gandharians have pale eyes.

Mother asked, measuring out her words, 'Why were you fighting with the Pandavas?'

'It was only with the fat boy,' I said.

I heard Dushasana sniffling. He was by the window, with Uncle Shakuni's arms around him. The servants had cleaned up the blood and dirt from our bodies, but the bump on his head was visible. One ear was red.

My own face hurt. The fat boy had grabbed Dushasana and banged his head against mine repeatedly. If I closed my jaws tight, I felt the bones grind under the swelling.

'Why did you fight with that boy?'

'He attacked Dushasana. In the elephant stalls.'

'In the elephant stalls?'

I should not have blurted that out. We were not allowed in the elephant stalls by ourselves.

'Haven't I told you to stay away from that boy?'

'Yes.'

'Then what were you doing with him?'

'I just went there to tell him something.'

'Tell him what?'

How could I answer that? The fat fool did not like us. We did not like him either. But his rudeness to everyone, even to Dushasana—did Mother wish I pretended I saw nothing?

When I remained silent, Mother said, 'Two against one, child?'

'*Three* against one,' said Uncle Shakuni. 'That charioteer's son was also with them. The mahouts told me Bhima gave them all a good thrashing!'

My face felt hot. Uncle Shakuni was smiling, as if it was a joke.

The fat boy had thrown himself at us without warning. I could still taste the dirt from the floor where we had all gone down. Mud mixed with dung and fodder.

But Uncle Shakuni was wrong about the charioteer's son. Karna had nothing to do with it; this was my fight.

'Karna took no part,' I said. 'He is not to be blamed—he was just there!'

When Mother spoke, it was to Uncle Shakuni. 'How did two sons of the strong Dhritarashtra lose to a lone Pandava?'

'They are children,' Uncle Shakuni said. 'They have much to learn.'

Mother did not respond. Getting up, she walked with measured steps towards the inner chamber. She turned towards us at the door.

'Many people have made many sacrifices for you children,' she said, looking straight at me.

Turning towards where Uncle Shakuni stood, she added, 'Let that all not be in vain.'

4

I climbed out of the arena on trembling legs, careful not to show the exhaustion on my face. The roar of the crowd, which had risen to a crescendo moments ago, was ebbing now.

As I made my way up to the Kaurava pavilion, the trumpets blared again, merging with the thud of drums. They must be about to announce the next contest.

Dushasana rushed to embrace me at the entrance. 'The brahmin did us wrong stopping the fight,' he said. 'You *had* him!'

Pushing through a crowd of well-wishers, I sank into a couch and reached for the water jug. Dushasana dampened a cloth in a basin with floating tulsi leaves and began to wipe the blood and perspiration from my face, talking excitedly.

'Your Jataka opening—oh! It took him ages to break through!' he was saying. 'You were magnificent, brother!'

When the acharyas had announced a demonstration day to display our weaponry skills, I had only been delighted. The word around the palace was that Bhima was my equal; there were some who even said he could best me with the mace. How wrong they all were!

I had not forgotten the incident in the elephant stalls. The fat fool would never catch me by surprise again, ever. I had grown in the years since. I am taller than the Pandava now. Faster and stronger, too.

In the martial arts classes we all took together every day, the acharyas trained the Pandavas separately. A few times, when they brought us together for demonstrations, I had crossed paths with the fat boy.

I had noticed a crowd grew around us quickly on such occasions. The acharyas never really let us fight, stepping in too soon, too often.

But I had the measure of the fat boy and he was not my equal.

The focus of our training had shifted in the last year, after Dronacharya's arrival. Dronacharya was not a kshatriya, but a brahmin who has taken up arms for some reason. He was the brother-in-law of Kripacharya, our own teacher.

Dronacharya and his son Ashwathama had arrived in Hastinapur one fine day. Next day, we learnt Grandfather Bhishma had appointed him our principal teacher.

Dronacharya had patience for only those who loved the bow. It was as if other weapons did not matter. The mace and hand-to-hand, I had heard him say many times, were for the commoners and the foresters.

I did not hold with that. Wasn't Jarasandha, the great king of Magadha, renowned for his skills in personal combat? And Balarama of the Yadavas, who could match him with the mace?

I did not hold with Dronacharya's treatment of Karna, either. Our acharya had refused to teach Karna because of his birth! Weapons are not for the sutas, the charioteers, he had said of Karna—Karna, who could make the bowstring sing!

Only on my insistence had he allowed Karna to attend the morning lessons with us again, though Dronacharya made it abundantly clear the 'suta putra' was to come nowhere near him or Ashwathama.

Dronacharya spent much time coaching the Pandavas, especially the third Pandava. He could not stop talking about Arjuna. It was obvious the acharya had his favourites; obvious, also, that he did not care much for my brothers and I.

Still, I was happy when the demonstration day dawned. Our acharya may not have had the good of the Kauravas at heart when he called for it, but it was the opportunity I had been waiting for.

A new stadium had been erected. Rulers of neighbouring places were invited. There would be other royals, renowned warriors, priests, thousands of commoners.

And they would all see that Duryodhana, the eldest son of Dhritarashtra, was second to no Pandava.

I was ready when Bhima, twirling his mace studded with iron, arrogantly called out for someone to demonstrate against. Before the acharyas could appoint a disciple, I had stood up and said for everyone to hear.

'I will be your adversary.'

There were eager cries from the spectators. Kripacharya hesitated and looked at Dronacharya. But when I ran down and vaulted into the arena, they both stepped back.

Picking a mace an attendant offered and tossing it into the air to test its balance, I looked up at the royal pavilion.

Sanjaya was whispering into Father's ear. Mother sat rigid, staring down through her blindfold. From the way she held her head, I could tell she was displeased. Perhaps Mother was fearful I would lose and bring her disgrace.

'The spectators must not be disappointed,' I said, turning to Bhima.

He had started in the Valita stance, as I knew he would. I had watched him in training. Dushasana and I had practiced the strikes and counterstrikes to his moves a thousand times.

I settled into Jataka.

When I attacked, he had sidestepped. I swung again, turning quicker than he expected. This time iron bit into iron. Sparks flew.

The crowd roared.

Pushing his mace away forcibly, I adopted another stance. Pratyaleeda. I parried his blow and stepped away to circle him, inviting him to attack my flank. I knew my opponent was strong; I needed to tire him a little.

Even though I could predict his every move, I was surprised by his speed and dexterity. I had expected the fat Pandava to be slower. Parrying a flurry of blows with some difficulty, I moved away, forcing him to follow.

The spectators were on their feet now, sensing this was no ordinary demonstration. I kept him at bay using my superior reach, darting in to harass him, then retreating quickly.

'Coward,' I heard him hiss. 'Stand your ground! Fight!!'

As the battle continued, I sensed his frustration. It was obvious he had underestimated me. Every time the spectators shouted, he attacked me with renewed energy. Every attack was slower than the one before. He was tiring.

I could feel my own breath rasping in my throat. The mace grew heavier with every blow. But when I thought of Mother's blindfolded eyes boring into my back, I knew I would not lose. I would go on till nightfall, if I had to.

I blinked away the sweat from my eyes and waited for his next attack. I let the first swing whistle past, parrying the next three, then yielded ground rapidly. Swinging his mace right and left in turns, he advanced.

When I gave ground again, dropping into a low lunge, he thought he had his chance. My mace was held low—too low to protect me.

I saw triumph in his eyes.

Roaring, he charged. I waited for him to lift his mace high for his last swing... to fully commit... it was but a moment's work for me then to twist away and cave in his ribs—now!

'Stop!'

Dronacharya had stepped swiftly forward to hold my mace hand. Several voices shouted at me. Ashwathama was shielding the Pandava.

One more moment. If only—

'Brother, that is—that is Karna!'

Dushasana's words broke into my thoughts. Vaguely, as my mind wandered, I had noted that Arjuna was demonstrating his skills below, earning loud applauses from the crowd.

But now another contestant had entered the arena —Karna!

I had not seen Karna for months. Not since Dronacharya announced the exhibition had he attended lessons or been near the palace.

Now, as I watched, he walked forward, and, casually, without seeming to aim, shot at the boar's head at one end. One by one the arrows Arjuna had fixed there fell, cut in half.

I jumped up, cheering. The spectators were on their feet.

Karna was not done. A stream of arrows flew from his bow again, arching high into the sky, then fell, vertically, to form a perfect swastika on the ground!

The crowd roared now. I roared over the commotion, 'Karna, I bow before you! The Kuru kingdom bows before you!'

When the noise settled, Karna turned to Arjuna, who was standing immobile. 'If we are done with childish tricks, I challenge you to a duel.'

Applause rocked the arena. But cries of protest rang down from the Pandava pavilion. 'Who let the suta putra in?' I heard Yudhistira ask. The acharyas looked agitated.

Sensing Karna might need help, I ran down into the arena, with Dushasana close behind. Arjuna, looking shaken, was mumbling some bravado to Bhima, who was now standing next to him.

Karna's face showed relief when he saw me. I moved quickly to his side. Helping him fasten his breastplate, I looked at the acharyas.

Dronacharya, his body soaked in perspiration, was saying something to Kripacharya. I noticed his wet sacred thread clinging to his body and wondered what use it had for a man who had embraced the warrior's way of life.

Kripacharya now hurried to where Arjuna stood. Placing a hand on the Pandava's shoulders, he faced the crowd. 'It is customary for opponents to be introduced before a duel. This is Prince Arjuna, son of King Pandu!'

Turning to Karna, Kripacharya asked, 'Who wishes to challenge him?'

I heard Karna's sharp intake of breath. He swallowed. 'I am Karna—son of Athiratha,' he said in a low voice.

'Athiratha of—? Arjuna is of the Kuru race. He will engage with any opponent of equal status. You must tell us your lineage.'

Karna's face was ashen. I trembled at the insult. Pushing forward, I bellowed for everyone to hear:

'Since when have we started mocking the brave? Since when has parentage saved a warrior on the battlefield? Do we not all die the same in combat?'

I said to the acharyas, more quietly, 'If Arjuna is unwilling to fight one who is not a king, I gift Karna the kingdom of Anga, which I inherited. From this moment, Karna is a king, worthy of any opponent here!'

Two priests came running to bless Karna. By the time they finished, my attention was drawn to a commotion. An old man, perspiring and clad in the clothes of a commoner, was trying to enter the arena. A guard blocked the way.

'Karna, where is Karna?' he said. 'They said he was hurt —where is my son?'

So this was Karna's father, Athiratha. Karna rushed to him.

'Father,' he said, bowing to touch the old man's feet. 'I am not hurt.'

Athiratha hugged Karna. The old man was sobbing. I heard derisive laughter from the Pandava supporters. Then I heard the fat boy:

'Just as a dog does not deserve butter, you do not deserve

the bow. The whip suits you better! But I will still fight, if any of Pandu's sons will do!'

Swiftly I turned to him. 'Think about your own parentage before you mock others!' I said. 'Just how did the eunuch Pandu have five sons, Bhima?'

Cursing, he charged at me, but Ashwathama stepped in between. Dronacharya was signalling furiously. Trumpets blared, signalling the end of the contest.

Slowly I approached Karna. Releasing himself from his father's embrace, he came forward. Holding his shoulders, I said, 'King of Anga, I salute you for your courage. You have my unending gratitude!'

Karna said quietly, 'I will not forget.'

5

There was silence in the room after the spy from Varanavata left. I did not trust myself to speak. I looked at Uncle Shakuni, who sat with his head bowed, absently playing with the dice carved out of ivory that never seemed to leave his person.

It was Dushasana who finally broke the silence. 'They must be stopped!' he said looking at me first, then Karna. 'We must send instructions!'

It was the month of Karthika. The spy, a Vaishya trader, had brought news of the Pandavas. They had been gone for a while from Hastinapur, ostensibly to attend the Pashupati festival that had commenced in Varanavata near the Madra region.

I was pleased when, after much deliberation and many consultations, Yudhistira had announced they would attend the festival this year. It would be a relief to have them out of the palace, even for a little while.

Trouble had been brewing for months. Every day our men brought whispers of conversations against us, of court-yard meetings and assemblages where my father's sightlessness came up. People had begun to question our right to rule!

The sons of Pandu had not been idle.

Uncle Shakuni was the first to point out that the journey to Varanavata was not innocent. The region had been a stronghold of Pandu in the olden days. There would be many there willing to pay obeisance to his sons.

The news the spy brought made me seethe. Far from partaking in the festivities, the Pandavas were cultivating loyalists. Yudhistira held long meetings with chieftains who arrived from Madra and nearby everyday. Many were now referring to him as the 'rightful heir'.

Uncle Shakuni stirred. He said, 'They will come back stronger.'

'I say we send the soldiers!' Dushasana said. 'Bring them to Hastinapur bound hand and foot!'

Uncle Shakuni looked at him impatiently. 'Is that the statecraft you have learnt from the brahmins?'

'But we cannot allow this! This is treachery!'

'Such confabulations are dangerous,' Uncle Shakuni said. 'But it is only natural for princes to meet their subjects.'

Like Dushasana, I ached to confront my cousins. This was worse than anything they had done in Hastinapur. I had no expectation of loyalty from my cousins, but to campaign against us with regional chieftains so brazenly!

But I knew Uncle Shakuni was right. The Pandavas had many supporters in Hastinapur. Not just among the people, but in the palace as well. Even the acharyas favoured them. We would not get far with a frontal approach.

'No, we must be astute,' Uncle Shakuni said. 'This is an opportunity—one we must use skilfully.'

'They must not be allowed back!' Dushasana said. 'Banish them!'

Uncle Shakuni shook his head. 'It would never be allowed. No, we need to be cleverer.'

Then he said, 'But you are right—they must not return.'

Silence. Uncle Shakuni stood up and began pacing.

'You must not forget Yudhistira's claim to the throne—' Dushasana was about to say something, but Uncle Shakuni continued. '—yes, I know that is a weak claim. But that is not how many people see it.'

Many people! By that I knew Uncle meant those among our elders who had engineered Pandu's ascendance to the Hastinapur throne, bypassing our father, his elder by birth. How can a blind man rule, they had asked.

But when King Pandu chose to depart for the forests discarding his duties to Hastinapur, the same elders had forgotten their objection. The blind man may rule now.

Then, years later, when the sons of Pandu had returned, how quickly they had changed! How quickly loyalties had switched! It occurred to me that the throne of Hastinapur had always been at the whim of fickle old men blinded by opportunism.

'Too many eyes watch over the Pandavas in Hastinapur,' Uncle Shakuni was saying. 'But misfortunes often befall travellers in distant lands—even princes. If something were to occur in Varanavata...'

Uncle Shakuni looked at me. He said, 'It is only a matter of time before there is unrest over who sits on the throne.'

I glanced at Karna. His expression was troubled. Sensing my unasked question, he said:

'Grant me leave to end this. I have a few scores to settle.'

'No!' Uncle Shakuni said. 'We cannot be involved—it must be achieved by other means.'

Other means. Deception. But then, in all the years I had known my cousins, when had they not meant me ill-will?

Perhaps seeing the look on my face, Uncle Shakuni approached me.

'I know this is not your way,' he said, 'but do not the scriptures say that the enemy must be overcome by any means necessary?

'Do they not say "by curses and incantations, by gift of wealth, by poison, or by deception, the foes should be slain?"'

Hearing my silence, Uncle Shakuni added, 'Allowing the enemy to acquire strength is not wise. It only invites more bloodshed.'

I let his words sink in. The past raged through me like an elephant in musth. Then, gathering my thoughts, I stood up and said to Dushasana:

'The dead cannot return. Send word to Varanavata.'

6

The words were polite, contrite—but not the look in her eyes.

Bold eyes locked on my face insolently, the Queen of Indraprastha begged my forgiveness for the morning's misfortune. She hoped I was not aggrieved. So did King Yudhistira.

'The marbles from Mainaka in the Garden Hall are mischievous,' said Draupadi. 'Perhaps our architect overextended himself there—it does take a keen eye to discern where the floor ends and water begins!'

In my mind, I cursed the infernal palace. I cursed its hidden pools and the devilish hands that built them. I cursed the queen who uttered words with withheld meanings.

But most of all, I cursed the Pandavas for not dying.

The word that came from Varanavata all those months ago was my cousins had perished in a fire. If I felt remorse at their death, it had not lasted long.

Later, the spies brought the news my cousins had survived. They had gone into hiding.

They had surfaced at the swayamvara of the Panchala princess, Draupadi, more than a year later. I remembered that occasion distinctly. The haughty princess had heaped insult on Karna, questioning his birth and refusing his suit!

Surprising everyone, King Drupada had married off his daughter to the Pandavas—not just to one, but to all!

Then had come the demand for a share of the kingdom, with Drupada's backing. Months of wrangling had followed, and in the end, we had negotiated a settlement I was not displeased with.

Hastinapur stayed with us.

The price we paid was the green forests and rolling mountains of the Khandava region in the south of the kingdom.

Months passed. Travellers brought tales of the city the Pandavas were building. They called it Indraprastha. Its centrepiece was a 'celestial' palace, which my cousins boasted would put Hastinapur to shame—fit for Indra himself to live!

When the invitation to visit Indraprastha came, I had hesitated. I did not like accepting Yudhistira's hospitality, but there was wisdom in Uncle Shakuni's advice that it was an opportunity to assess the new king's strengths.

And Indraprastha? We found little at fault with the city itself. In its first flush, it was bustling with traders, artisans and settlers from as far as Khamboja. But the palace was nothing like what it was made out to be.

It was built to impress, with a great number of golden columns, ornate archways, and crystal-studded corridors that wandered into grand but purposeless halls. There were stairways made of ivory. There were concealed doors, camouflaged doorways.

I wondered how much of Yudhistira's inheritance had been poured into the palace, which shone with the untempered artistry of newfound wealth.

And pools! The place was full of confounded pools! Earlier, on the last day of my visit, I had slipped and fallen into one. There was laughter, even among the servants!

Now, to rub in my humiliation, Draupadi herself had arrived, with her retinue of maids.

'I am told that many find the Garden Hall difficult to navigate,' she said. 'The marbles have been brought up from the very bottom of Bindusaras—people say they change colour to reflect the good thoughts of the beholder!'

Draupadi searched my face. Was she looking for good thoughts? It irked me to see her maids were staring too.

Drawing a deep breath, I said the Garden Hall was indeed exquisite.

'Often, I am told, visitors misread the floor and get a drenching,' Draupadi continued. 'I trust the Prince suffered no injury?'

None, I assured her.

'Allow me to send for the physician at least—if not for anything, to ease my conscience.'

More pleasantries from the Queen. She asked after the comforts of my party—Uncle Shakuni and the others who had accompanied me, she hoped everyone was being looked after?

Then, reminding me of the entertainment that had been laid out in the Game Hall that night, she departed, leaving behind a faint fragrance of lotus.

Good thoughts, the Queen had said.

Witnessing my indignity from the balcony in the morning, I wondered what thoughts had made the Queen whisper to her maids that not just the king of Hastinapur was blind.

I had not missed their merriment.

7

The white gates of Indraprastha had hardly disappeared behind us when Uncle Shakuni leaned forward.

'We must invite them to Hastinapur,' he said. 'Soon.'

The previous night's revelries had caught up with Dushasana and he had chosen to travel by himself. So we had the chariot to ourselves.

I looked at Uncle Shakuni, who said, 'Courtesy demands it. Yes.'

My uncle was not one to act for the sake of courtesy alone. I waited. He was silent for a while, looking out at the gold of the barley fields that stretched out on both sides. Abruptly, he turned to me.

'What did you notice most at Indraprastha?'

'That palace must have eaten up half their treasury,' I said. 'Yudhistira is a fool! To spend on vanity when he does not have a proper army!'

'Perhaps not as much as you think. What else?'

'They have allies. More than our spies reported. I had not expected so many at the ceremony.'

'Yes. There were many minor kings—don't forget the minor kings. Sometimes opulence breeds obeisance. People are easily fooled.'

It was true. There were rulers from Kirata, Vanga, Pandrya and many territories beyond the Vindhyas. Some were not more than mere tribal chieftains, but there were more sovereigns than I cared to count and they had all pledged allegiance.

'That Yadava brought them together,' Uncle Shakuni said. 'Yudhistira could not have done it—it was Krishna, I am certain.'

Krishna of Dwaraka was a maternal relative of the Pandavas. Years ago, I had spent several summers at his palace, learning mace warfare from Balarama, his famed elder brother. While Balarama was most affectionate, Krishna had pretended I did not exist.

'By my sums, Indraprastha now has a treasury that matches ours,' Uncle Shakuni said. 'Those new allegiances have brought in much in the way of gold and gifts.'

Uncle Shakuni fell silent. A while later he asked, 'What did you notice about the Pandavas?'

'Bhima looked the same. Sullen and insolent, just as I expected. As for Yudhistira, his sermons have become more insufferable! All that talk about truth and honesty and duty—yet I wouldn't put it past him to bend the truth to his will!'

Uncle Shakuni nodded. 'What else?'

I tried to remember. More than Yudhistira's pompous conduct in public, what stuck in my mind was his fleshy face, red with wine and shiny with sweat, poring over the dice board in the Game Hall. I had played a few hands with him, on his insistence.

I said, 'Gambler. He lives for it. And he drinks—a lot.'

'I noticed. He does not seem to be able to control his weaknesses.'

Uncle Shakuni leaned back in his seat. He closed his eyes.

He said, 'We must invite the king to Hastinapur.'

8

A fterwards, when it was all over, when the threats had been made, the tears shed, and the last dice rolled, I would wonder about the silence of my elders.

Why did they, the wise men of my clan, not say a word till it was too late?

What was their gamble?

But then, in that moment when time stretched to eternity and back and the dice rattled and lay still on the ivory board, all I could do was marvel at the mindlessness of Yudhistira.

The madness that must have seized him!

When we invited Yudhistira to Hastinapur, I had thought he might demur. But he had accepted with alacrity. And on the night of his arrival, as the ceremonial banquet ended, he had sighed contentedly turning to me.

'If your after-dinner diversion is as good as your feast, I must say I will be very pleased, Duryodhana!' he said, smiling. 'I hear you have built a new gaming hall?'

Later, in the entertainment hall after we had all taken our seats, Yudhistira had nodded absently when I said Uncle Shakuni would play in my stead. He rubbed his hands and looked around the room, smiling at the assemblage.

Father was there in his appointed seat, with Grandfather Bhishma, Drona and Kripa seated nearby. Father's attendant, Sanjaya, stood behind. My brothers and the invited kings had gathered around as well.

With Dushasana and Karna, I had taken a seat behind Uncle Shakuni. Over his shoulder, I saw Yudhistira's eager face, and behind them, the other Pandavas. They looked displeased. Bhima stared at me darkly.

Yudhistira had won the throw to start the game.

Then he began to lose.

As his losses mounted, the smile left Yudhistira's face. He ignored the protests of his brothers and raised the stakes. He called for more wine. Twice he interrupted our throw to inspect the dice, complaining the game was rigged.

'Let's stop,' Uncle Shakuni said at one point, when much of Indraprastha's treasury rested with us. 'We need not continue.'

Yudhistira snapped. 'I will not withdraw, Shakuni, Son of Soubala! Unlike some here, my means are unlimited!'

I saw Uncle Shakuni's back stiffen. I hoped anger would not cloud his judgement. But I need not have worried.

Mesmerised, I watched as Yudhistira decimated himself. When the gold and jewels were gone, he pledged his servants and soldiers. After that, the palace and the land. Then the elephants and livestock.

Then he pledged his brothers, one by one.

And in four swift throws lost them all.

The pledge for the last throw, the one we all watched breathlessly now, had been himself.

The dice rattled and came to rest. The minister appointed to call out the results hesitated.

Uncle Shakuni's quiet voice cut into the silence.

'I have won.'

9

Yudhistira slumped back, closing his eyes. After a while, perhaps feeling everyone was looking at him, he struggled to his feet, using the dice table for support.

He stood there, swaying, an old man all of a sudden. Abruptly he sat down, slapping the edge of the board and making the dice jump.

'I am not finished yet!' he roared. 'I have one more piece of wealth—Draupadi, my wife, equal in beauty to Goddess Lakshmi herself!'

The hall rang with cries of protest. I saw Bhima jump to his feet shouting angrily, but Yudhistira did not even look at him.

Uncle Shakuni turned to me. He looked tired.

It looked like the night had gotten away from us.

'If I win, I take back everything—my country, my palace, my brothers, everything!' Yudhistira was saying. 'I pledge my dearest wife, Draupadi herself—let's play!'

I heard Karna draw in a sharp breath. Dushasana held

my arm and said, 'No, brother! Why risk all that we have won?'

I stood up. Yudhistira's eyes were fixed on me. There was no vanity, no hubris, in them now—only fear and desperation...and hate.

Was this the same resplendent king of Indraprastha who walked into this hall? The righteous ruler who worshipped morality? How swift the downfall! How quickly morality crumbled!

And now, he wanted one more game, one last chance, to win back everything, to right the night's many wrongs! And for that, one more immoral pledge!

Was it right to allow him that? Where did morality stand now?

Not knowing what I wanted, I looked at Yudhistira. Let fate decide!

I said, 'I accept.'

A babble of voices erupted around me. Some were of protest. Others laid bets of their own. I did not care.

The dice rattled. Once. Then a second time.

Silence roared.

Uncle Shakuni's voice rang out again.

'Deceit!' Yudhistira snarled.

10

Everyone was talking all at once. After his utterance, Yudhistira sank into himself. The other Pandavas were on their feet, arguing. I felt Dushasana and Karna move to my side.

'You cheated!' one of the Pandava twins shouted. 'One day I will kill you for this, Shakuni—I swear, in front of everyone here!'

'Quiet! Nobody cheated!' I yelled. 'And nobody forced your brother to place insane bets!'

As the noise in the hall died down, I looked around the room. There was disbelief on some faces, anger on others— delight, too.

My eyes rested on the elders. Vidura looked upset. Father was listening to Sanjaya. Grandfather Bhishma looked ahead, expressionless. So did Drona and Kripa. Nobody met my eyes.

Turning to Yudhistira, I said, 'Take off your finery. It is not right for servants to wear them.'

Wordlessly Yudhistira stood up and began to remove his

upper cloth. He folded it neatly and placed it on the dice table.

Karna said to me, 'Where is Draupadi? Ask her to be brought here! Let her stand with her husbands!'

I saw the King of Anga's flushed face and remembered the humiliation he had faced at Draupadi's swayamvara. Many had jeered when she refused to allow him to compete for her hand, questioning his birth. Karna had not forgotten.

'Stop this madness!

I looked around. Vidura stood before Father, shaking.

'This son will burn Hastinapur to the ground! It was not for nothing that jackals howled when he was born! Stop him before he destroys the Kuru clan!'

Vidura, who ate our salt, but favoured the sons of Pandu! Never had I heard him say but a deprecating word about us! Where was his rage when the virtuous Yudhistira staked morality?

Ignoring him, I walked to the dice table. The Pandavas stood behind it, bare-chested, glowering. Shaking off Arjuna's restraining hand, Bhima pointed a trembling finger at me.

'You will die for this treachery, Duryodhana! For this, I will break your bones and crush your skull! Make no mistake—it is I, Bhimasena, who says so in front of all here!'

I looked at him silently. I heard his contemptuous voice heaping insults at us all through the years. And I heard the merriment in Indraprastha, the laughter of the queen with haughty eyes.

I said for everyone to hear, 'Bring Draupadi.'

11

The sentries stiffened at their posts when I stepped out into the south courtyard of the palace. A few servants stood around talking in a corner. Seeing me, they quickly melted away.

I stood there for a while, breathing in the chill of the Karthika month. Lights shone through many windows, including my own. Not many in the palace would sleep tonight.

Crossing the courtyard, I passed between two sentries into the south wing and climbed the stairs to my quarters. Ghee lamps flickered in the outer hall, though there was no one there.

I hesitated, undecided whether to go into the bed chamber, then sat down on a diwan. The conches for dawn would sound soon, followed by the trumpet call for weapons training. I did not want to miss the morning practice. Besides, I did not think I could sleep.

Footsteps from inside. She stood in the doorway, my bride for eternity, glorious as golden dusk even when roused from sleep. Bhanumati had not changed since I first set eyes on her at her swayamvara in the Kalinga palace. Nobody would say she had borne twins.

'Have they left?' she asked.

'Yes.'

'Where to?'

'The forests. Twelve years in exile, then one year living incognito. If they are recognised in that one year, it is exile for another twelve years. That's the penalty agreed on.'

'Draupadi?'

'The exile only applied to the Pandavas. But she chose to go with her husbands.'

Nobody could have foreseen the chain of events that unfolded tonight. Such recklessness from Yudhistira! And my Father, the King—how could he throw away all we had won, all our advantages, with one tremulous pronouncement at the whiff of a woman's tears?

I had not heard what Draupadi said to Father when she fell at his feet. But I had been furious when he—he who had sat silent all through the night!—suddenly announced the Pandavas were free. Unconditionally!

Not just that. They would retain half their stakes, including Indraprastha! Between Draupadi's tears and Vidura's whispers, Father had arrived at a most unwise decision. Did he really think the Pandavas would go back and live peacefully after their humiliation?

But when Uncle Shakuni suggested another game, Yudhistira had not been able to resist. Perhaps he imagined redeeming himself and returning to Indraprastha in glory, with more treasury than he left. Perhaps there was no escape for a gambler.

Whatever his thoughts, Yudhistira had sat down again.

And again, he had lost.

'The servants brought me news in the first quarter of the

night,' Bhanumati said. 'There was talk of deceit at the game.'

'Losers' talk!'

It irked me the canard was spreading. Deceit? The upstart Yudhistira will need to be reborn to beat Uncle Shakuni at the dice board!

Bhanumati took a step forward and stopped. I sensed the unease in her and knew what she was going to say.

'I heard some terrible pledges were made.'

Bhima. When Draupadi had refused to come to the hall, Dushasana had brought her in forcibly. Bhima had thumped himself on the chest then and proclaimed he would kill Dushasana—and drink his blood.

'They all made pledges. To kill us in various ways. But nobody did anything.'

'Why did you allow it? To drag a woman to a room full of men—and in her state!'

I had noticed the blood on Draupadi's waist cloth, the red that fell between her feet on the white marble.

'You should have stopped Dushasana—you know how impulsive he is!'

'Dushasana is not to fault. It was me. I gave the order.'

I felt Bhanumati draw in a deep breath. She got up and was silent. Then she said, 'Can you blame Bhima? What if—what if it had been me?'

'If it were you,' I said, gazing up, 'I wouldn't have pledged —I would have killed and drank blood right there!'

Bhanumati looked at me for a long moment. There was anger on her face, tenderness...and more sorrow than I ever cared to see. Then, without a word, she disappeared inside.

None of this was meant to happen, I wanted to scream after her. No one was meant to gamble a kingdom, or brothers, or wife!

I don't know how long I sat there. I looked up sensing someone in the room. Mother. She was alone, no maid to guide her.

I stood up.

'If you have come to give me grief,' I said, 'I am ready.'

'Grief? No. Some bad decisions were made tonight. But also a good one.'

I waited.

'We would be preparing for war tomorrow if the Pandavas had returned to Indraprastha. The exile was a good solution.'

'War might still come to us,' I said. 'Drupada will not take this lightly.'

'No. Yudhistira agreed to the exile. Drupada is wise enough to know he cannot do much without the Pandavas.'

The aged Drupada might counsel patience, but his son, Dhrishtadyumna, might have other ideas.

'Not surprising that the King here acted with no fore-thought!' Mother was saying. 'One day perhaps he might listen to a counsel who does not have the welfare of Pandavas at heart. One day he might do what is good for the kingdom instead!'

She added as an afterthought, 'Or perhaps not. For the Kurus, statecraft ends with conquests and annexations and forced marriages. Then they go back to their petty wars and wine and palace maids!'

I kept my silence, unsure what to say. Mother sighed. Then she said softly, 'Do you know why I wear this blind-fold? There is much here I wish not to see—many faces!'

Turning, she moved towards the door. I rushed to open it. Mother stepped into the empty corridor slowly.

'Mother?'

She stopped.

'What did you come to tell me—what must I do?'

Mother looked back.

'Rule!' she said. 'Rule like the king Hastinapur has never had! You have thirteen years to erase this night—thirteen years to erase the memory of the sons of Pandu!'

12

A nd so I ruled, from the throne of my father, the kingdom forgotten by the king. Far too long it had been left in the hands of indifferent ministers and self-serving vassals. Far too long we had heard nothing from beyond the walls of Hastinapur than what we were meant to hear.

I travelled. Sometimes in company, most times alone. Unseen, I saw the land of my ancestors, the plains of the Purus and the coast beyond the Vindhyas, the land King Bharat brought together, the land his sons, my fathers, broke into tiny little pieces, to rule and misrule. I travelled to Gandhara and Khamboja in the north; in the south I went as far as Kumari, to the very end of land.

I saw the kingdoms Grandsire Bhishma annexed and never administered, the alliances he formed and never fostered. I walked amidst anger and angst; I walked among my people.

I ruled.

We heard of the Pandavas occasionally. First from Kamyaka, then from Dwaitavana. We heard of their move to

Badari. After that they crossed the Prasvarna ranges into Kailasa. Later, in the 12th year, they returned to Kamyaka. A few times our men clashed with them during cattle-drives.

Then they disappeared.

Our spies scoured the earth. Panchala, Kosala, Salva, Videha, Kalinga, Magadha, even Anga and Gandhara. Then word came from Matsya, from the court of King Virata.

It was the last month of the last year of their exile when we marched into Matsya from the north. I watched as our soldiers clashed and my cousins revealed themselves on the battlefield.

This was the thirteenth year—the year they should have remained unrecognised.

13

Insolence dripped from Krishna's lips, like perspiration from a wrestler's brow. He addressed Father directly.

'King Dhritarashtra, I have come to prevent the destruction of your race,' he said. 'Your sons have taken from the Pandavas what is rightfully theirs by unjust means. You know that. Prevail on them to return to the sons of Pandu their share of the kingdom!'

Dushasana muttered something angrily from behind me. The previous messenger from the Pandavas had made the same demand as Krishna—only more diplomatically. Surely these were not the best words from a man come for peace?

Since our discovery of the Pandavas in their year of hiding, messengers had gone back and forth. The brahmin they sent first insisted the Pandavas had completed their exile, conveniently pointing to the lunar calendar.

When our astrologers countered with the error of that calculation, the brahmin had said no more. A messenger went from our side to Virata as well. Then had come Krishna to Hastinapur.

He had made it a point to offend from the moment he arrived. He had rejected our hospitality, refusing to stay at the palace or even dine with us. This morning he had barely allowed for the salutations to be over before making his discourteous demand.

Father cleared his throat. He said, 'It is true that war will cause great destruction. Both sides are strong and there will be countless deaths. But my son rules now. I am powerless.'

Krishna regarded me with disdain—the same disdain he had shown me all those years ago when I had stayed at Dwaraka—and began to speak. I was conscious all eyes were on me.

'Listen to me, Duryodhana,' he said. 'The Pandavas met the conditions that you set, even though it was by deceit that you took their kingdom. Yet you still refuse to keep your word! Shed this sinfulness. Give back their kingdom!'

Dushasana spoke. 'The Pandavas did not meet the conditions! They were found out before their time ended! Let them roam the forests for another 13 years before they come to stake claim!'

'Perhaps you are not aware of the extra months that accrue every four years,' Krishna said. 'According to the lunar calendar—'

I did not let him finish.

'We will accept the lunar calculations, if you insist,' I said. 'But that also means the incognito year began five months earlier. What were the Pandavas doing in Kamyaka in plain sight during that time, Krishna? Should they not have been in hiding?'

Krishna looked at the elders. 'This son of yours will destroy Hastinapur. Why does he hold such enmity towards his cousins? Make him see sense—prevent slaughter!'

Grandsire Bhishma said something about the need for

brothers to live together harmoniously. Dronacharya made a similar speech. Then Vidura turned a displeased face towards me.

'You think you have the might to win this war,' he said. 'You don't.

'You will only bring death to all of you—and I say that not for your sake, but for the sake of your parents. For the sin of having brought such a wicked son into this world, they will have to wander the earth in sorrow in their old age!'

I stood up. I had had enough of the wisdom of the elders.

'You find fault with me alone for all this! Where was your wisdom when Yudhistira was staking his kingdom, his brothers, his wife? Where was your wisdom when he gambled away all that was his, *twice,* like a mad man?

'Now you chastise me for not letting him rule! Is such a man fit to be king? Tell me, why should our people be subjected to him?'

I stopped to tame my breathing. Looking at Vidura, I continued more calmly.

'You speak of my defeat. I will not be defeated. So long as I have Karna and Drona and Kripa and Grandsire Bhishma, who has sworn to protect this throne, I will not be defeated. And if I am, so I will gladly die on the battlefield— like a true kshatriya!'

Into the silence that engulfed the court hall drifted more of Krishna's poison. 'You seem to desire a death on the battlefield, Duryodhana! Make no mistake, you and your advisers will get the deaths you deserve!'

I turned to face Krishna. With infinite restraint, I walked down to where he sat. As far as I was concerned, the negotiations were over.

'As long as I live, I will surrender no part of this kingdom to the Pandavas,' I told him.

'Not even a needlepoint.'

14

On the eve of battle, a military camp quietens down in a particular order.

There is a phase where the noise is at its loudest, when men who know they may not see another sunset sit around fire-pits and overindulge, cloaking their fear in boisterous bravado. After that peak, sounds begin to fade—slowly, imperceptibly, at first; then swiftly, urgently.

I listened to the darkness at Kurukshetra. The camp had fallen into an uneasy slumber a long time ago. Occasionally I heard the sentries outside the palace tent—the clank of metal, a hurried conversation, footsteps.

Do kings sleep before battle? I doubted it.

The Pandavas had set up camp on the western side of the field. We had the east. Behind us flowed the mighty Hiranvati. On the lower banks, where the river curved, we had marked out a large site covered with rocks and thorny bushes for our crematorium.

Armies of this scale had never clashed before. What I knew of the biggest war so far, the Battle of Ten Kings in which our ancestor King Sudas defeated the northerners, paled when compared to the forces that we had amassed.

The Pandavas had seven divisions fighting for them. Against that, we had eleven. That gave us the advantage in numbers. But how far could one rely on the army of others?

The soldiers from Dwaraka and Madra, they were reluctant recruits. The men from Dwaraka joined our ranks only because of Balarama, who, having decided he would not fight, felt compelled to offer his army instead. And the Madra soldiers were with us because we had not allowed King Shalya to forget the many debts he owed Hastinapur.

And the acharyas, how would they fight? They cared for the Pandavas more than us. Arjuna is dearer to me than my own son, wasn't that what Drona had said all those years ago, at the skills exhibition? How far would the old brahmin go against the disciple dearer than his own blood?

Then there was Grandsire Bhishma himself. He had never hidden the fact he favoured the sons of Pandu, the warrior king, to the sons of Dhritarashtra, the blind king. Would he steel his heart to destroy the Pandavas?

Already the elders had done harm with their stubbornness. The grandsire, who had assumed supreme command of our forces, had refused to allow Karna on the battlefield. The acharyas had only been happy to support him—for them, Karna was still the son of the charioteer!

Karna had smiled when he heard of the stipulation. Only, I saw the hurt in his eyes. I will wait, he had said. Tell me when the old men are done, when you need me.

So we had sat down without Karna, the most able of my commanders, to agree on the rules of combat with the enemy.

Battle would commence at sunrise, end at sunset.

Fighting should be between equals—chariot fighters, for

example, should engage chariot fighters only, not foot soldiers.

Weapons must not be used against the injured or those who had lost their arms or breastplates.

Weapons must not be used against charioteers and drummers.

The surrendered must not be mistreated.

Those who wish to withdraw from battle should be allowed to do so.

Corpses must not be mutilated.

We had reiterated to each other the rules of righteous war every warrior knows by heart, knowing also in our hearts that once bloodshed began rules and righteousness would be wisps in the wind.

That was the way of wars. They were too wild to bind by rules, too beastly to tame by morality. Wars did not discern between the good and bad, the firm and infirm, the young and old. Wars killed the king and the commoner alike.

I thought of the tens of thousands who had assembled at Kurukshetra. This was once a holy site for our ancestors, where King Kuru performed his ascetic austerities. How ironic his successors would now use it as a site for excesses!

How many of us will leave this battlefield? Of the kings and chieftains and tribals and commoners who will fight tomorrow, how many will survive?

Will the elders live through this, the grandsire, Drona, Kripa, Bahlika?

Who among my generation will walk away from Kuruk-shetra? Dushasana, Vikarna, Ashwathama, Somadatta, Jayadratha...Karna?

And our sons, those children of fifteen and sixteen, come to fight their fathers' war! How many will live through tomorrow?

I looked at the slight form by the doorway. Laxmana, my gentle son with his mother's eyes—for whom war was but a game. How peacefully he sleeps!

Will he survive?

I closed my eyes. The night marched on without mercy.

15

I t rained again that morning. Water had pooled in the low-lying areas, curtailing the battlefield. Men fought in mud, bathed in the stench of the dead, amidst rotting corpses and bloated carcasses that the scavengers were yet to remove.

I fought mindlessly. Once I clashed with Yudhistira, who quickly withdrew in favour of Bhima. I had engaged Bhima from the chariot several times since the war began. Always, I had longed to pick up the mace and jump out to settle our old score. But that was not prudent for a king.

Disengaging from Bhima, I returned to the middle ranks soon. Messengers kept arriving with news from the other fronts.

Susarman was weakening against Arjuna and needed support. The young Sushena, Karna's son, was waging a spirited battle against Uttamauja. Kripa was engaging Shikhandi. Kritavarma had taken on Nakula. I heard with joy Karna was spreading like wildfire amidst the Panchalas.

The rain stopped. The sun shone with a vengeance.

Noting Uncle Shakuni's banner near Bhima's division, I ordered the charioteer to the front again.

The Gandhara formation lay in tatters. Uncle Shakuni's bodyguards had been killed and he faced Bhima from his chariot. He looked exhausted. I saw he had been pierced several times.

When I cut in with three eagle-feathered arrows, Bhima turned his attention to me. Ignoring the shafts that darted around me like wasps, I took my time. My first missile clanked against the metal of his flagpole. But the second found its mark, piercing his breastplate.

Quickly stringing another arrow, I sighted carefully. I would make this count.

Bhima suddenly let his bow clatter to the deck. Picking up his mace, he vaulted to the ground, roaring. As the ground troops scattered, I saw my bodyguards moving in to intercept. The Virata soldiers, who were protecting Bhima, surged forward.

I felt my hand reaching for my own mace...

'Don't—don't be provoked!' my charioteer shouted, swinging away to avoid being flanked. 'The war will be over if you are captured!'

As he whipped the horses to give me distance, a ring of chariots came into view. Dushasana. With him were Dundadhara, Dhanurgraha and Shanda. I had thought my brothers were in the northern front, with Karna.

'Leave him, brother,' Dushasana shouted. 'I will send him where he belongs!'

The sun had climbed high and was beginning its descent. I drove towards the rest area, where messengers were waiting.

Kripa had half-killed Shikhandi. Ashwathama had defeated Satyaki and Dhrishtadyumna. Yudhistira was fool enough to engage Karna directly, but had somehow escaped.

News came in quick succession. Sushena had fallen. So had Vrasasena, Karna's eldest.

Vrasasena had been killed by Arjuna. Karna had heard. He was attacking Arjuna.

Ignoring the attendants tending to my wounds, I jumped up. The charioteer ran off to bring the vehicle around. I tried not to think of the fallen. It served no purpose.

When a horseman from the northern sector rushed in and stood panting, I knew something ominous had happened.

Karna was dead!

I sat down, suddenly empty.

When I looked up, the camp had fallen silent. The messenger had blurted out the devastating news and rushed away. The attendants stood around, disbelief on every face.

It was only when Shalya returned that we got to know what happened.

The Madra king, renowned for his horsemanship, had driven Karna today. He had been reluctant to be Karna's charioteer and had agreed only when I pointed out there was no other who could match the skills of Krishna, who was driving Arjuna.

Shalya spoke of how Karna had decimated the troops protecting Arjuna's flanks. When Karna challenged Arjuna, everyone had stopped to watch. Vijaya, the great bow that rarely left Karna's hands, was unerring today, against Arjuna's Gandiva.

The two had fought a dazzling duel, astounding everyone with their speed of hand. 'Several times Arjuna should have fallen,' Shalya said. 'It was Krishna's skills that saved him.'

Just before his death, as he strung a serpent-headed arrow, Shalya had told Karna to aim for Arjuna's chest instead of his head. Karna had scoffed, saying the chest was for old men who couldn't see their target.

Krishna had done something with the steeds, dropping them to their knees, and the arrow had passed, knocking off Arjuna's battle crown. Shalya muttered something about the arrogance of youth.

I listened with disbelief as Shalya narrated Karna's fall.

As the duel progressed, the chariots continued to circle each other. One of the wheels of Karna's vehicle had sunk into a rut. Shalya had struggled to pull out the chariot through muddy ground. Requesting time, as per the rules of war, Karna had jumped out to help.

Arjuna had felled him just as Karna was putting his shoulder to the wheel.

Shalya said, 'He did not deserve that death.'

I had nothing to say to that. After a while, Shalya said, 'I had not wanted to drive him—I had not wanted to drive a suta putra. I am glad I did. He fought like a king.'

I rose. Karna still lay where he fell.

16

We held no war council that night. It was not needed.

Uncle Shakuni came to me when I returned from the burial ground. We sat across each other, in distant worlds, waging losing wars against our own demons from behind a wall of silence.

I thought of the beginning, the first sunrise when our armies faced each other. War had looked glorious then. But that euphoria died quickly, as the dead piled up.

Of our eleven divisions, only a few hundred soldiers remained now. I doubted if the Pandavas had more. On both sides, the list of fallen heroes had grown long.

Grandsire Bhishma was the first to fall. Srutayudha, Shusharma, Bhagadatta, Bhurisravas, Dronacharya, all had followed quickly. And—

Uncle Shakuni spoke. 'Tomorrow I will die.'

I looked at him. The ghee lamps approaching the end of their lives flickered, etching deep shadows on Uncle Shakuni's face. I noticed streaks of white in his hair and beard that I had never seen before.

'I will fall to Nakula.'

Uncle Shakuni said it quietly but with certainty. It did not surprise me. Seventeen days of war had underlined the inevitability of death to all of us. It was the single constant from which there was no escape. But it held no sway over me now.

I remembered the night I lit Laxmana's pyre. The night I wept. I remembered lighting more pyres since then, for my fallen brothers.

Today it was Karna's...and Dushasana's. I had shed no tear today, I had not grieved—not even when I saw Dushasana's chest that Bhima had crushed. Onlookers said the Pandava had splashed his face with my brother's blood and laughed.

'Let Shalya lead tomorrow,' Uncle Shakuni broke into my thoughts again. 'Under the circumstances, he will make a better commander than Ashwathama or me.'

He rose. I, too, stood up. As he turned to leave, words spilled from me, without consent.

'How could this be?'

It was a few moments before Uncle Shakuni responded.

'Could we have avoided this war? Perhaps. But could you have made peace with the fact that you have given in to the evil of Yudhistira?'

He continued, 'Grandsire Bhishma should never have fallen. Dronacharya should never have been killed by Dhrishtadyumna, who was not his equal. And Karna— Arjuna could never have killed him!

'Yet all these happened. These cannot be undone. To dwell on the past, to wish for a different outcome, is not the conduct of a kshatriya. Your duty is to fight the enemy, to the best of your ability—to the last of your breath.'

Perhaps seeing the questions on my face, Uncle Shakuni added gently.

'Do not grieve for Dushasana, do not mourn Karna. Remember what the scriptures say? Death is but the soul changing old clothes—it is not the end, just the beginning of a new chapter in the eternal circle of life.'

It looked as if Uncle Shakuni wanted to say more. Instead he made his way to the exit. He stood there for a long moment, then turned to me.

'There is something you must know. Karna—he should have been fighting on the Pandava side. Not ours.'

I looked at him uncomprehendingly.

Uncle Shakuni said, 'We know Karna as the suta putra, the son of Athiratha. He wasn't. He was Kunti's firstborn. The child she bore while a maiden and cast away in shame!'

Karna was the eldest Pandava—heir to the kingdom!

I asked, after a while, 'Karna knew?'

Uncle Shakuni nodded.

'Krishna made sure of that. The day he visited Hasti-napur before the war, he met Karna. He tried to persuade Karna to join the Pandavas—offered him the throne of Hastinapur.

'Kunti, too, begged him. But Karna refused. He said you were more his brother than the Pandavas. The only conces-sion he granted Kunti was that he would only engage Arjuna—he would spare her other sons... I thought you should know.'

Uncle Shakuni left. I sank under the crushing weight of thoughts that raced trumpeting through my mind like maddened elephants.

I thought of the boy who had glowed like the Sun and decimated Arjuna in the skills demonstration all those years ago. I thought of his quiet words when I had stood by his side. I will not forget, Karna had said then.

I wept.

EPILOGUE

It must have been the soft thud of hooves on the forest trail that woke me. Through the athangali trees that stretch on to the shore, I watch three chariots drawing near and coming to a stop on the lakeside.

Men alight. I hear muffled conversation. Then, Yudhistira's excited voice.

'He must be here somewhere. These swamps are full of hiding places. The coward, he will not come out—we must shame him!'

I sit up quietly.

Another voice joins in. Krishna. I fail to catch what he says, but Yudhistira speaks up.

'Duryodhana! It is I, Yudhistira! Show yourselves—come out!'

Footfall. Men spreading out along the shore, looking for me. Again, I hear Yudhistira.

'Destroyer of the clan! Are you hiding? Come out! Either vanquish us and rule—or sleep your eternal sleep!'

I say, 'I am here.'

Sudden silence. Then a babble of voices, flurry of footsteps. A cluster of figures come into view. They are all there, the Pandavas and Krishna. Dhrishtadyumna, too, and Satyaki.

Yudhistira pushes his way forward. I realise he cannot see me when he calls out in my general direction.

'Be a man and face us! Where's your valour? Finish this righteous war!'

Unable to contain myself, I respond.

'Righteous war! Where was your righteousness when you killed the unarmed Karna? You lie and cheat and kill, yet you talk about valour! Is it valour that makes you challenge someone wounded—someone who has left the battlefield?'

Yudhistira retorts, louder than ever, 'I will not let you escape! Come out and fight for your kingdom!'

'You keep the kingdom!' I say, goading him further. 'What good will it be to me now? My son, my brothers, my relatives—all are dead! You can rule now!'

Yudhistira steps closer and calls out, 'I will not take the kingdom without defeating you! Choose your weapon. Fight any one of us—if you win, you keep the kingdom!'

In the silence that follow, I hear Krishna curse. He rages at Yudhistira.

'Is there no end to your stupidity? To make such a grand pronouncement! What if he challenges you or Arjuna or Nakula or Sahadeva for a mace fight? Perhaps the sons of Kunti are destined to roam the forests for ever!'

For a moment I toy with the idea of challenging Yudhistira. It would be child's play to cave in his skull—at least, Hastinapur would be rid of a man who should never be king.

Then I hear Bhima's voice.

'Fight me, Duryodhana! We have some old scores to

settle. I am the one who killed Dushasana and drank his blood. I promised I would kill all of Dhritarashtra's sons— you are the only one left!'

I think of the first day I faced off with Bhima, that hot morning of our childhood at the skills demonstration. Could all this have happened if I had killed him then? If only Dronacharya had not intervened!

I remember his pledge in the assembly hall and the broken bodies I had placed on the pyre every day for eighteen days and the crushed chest of Dushasana. I remember his contempt for Karna, the taunts of suta putra.

'Let's settle scores,' I say.

Then, gripping my mace, I crawl out of the swamp for my final fight.

ACKNOWLEDGMENTS

My deepest gratitude to:

Ananthan Prem, Asavari Singh, and Ayyappan R, for keeping me on the straight and narrow with my writing.

Liz Thorsen, Brad Gyori, and Vaiju Naravane for their comments on the the first draft.

The followers of @epicretold.

And, as always, my wife Svetlana Urupina for her infinite patience.

ABOUT THE AUTHOR

Before he embraced the serene life of an academic in UK, Chindu Sreedharan worked as a journalist in New Delhi, Mumbai, and New York. He lives in Bournemouth, a beautiful town on the southern coast of England, with his wife Svetlana.

A former competitive ballroom dancer with two British national titles to his name, his new passion is hiking. He is currently working on a non-fiction, *One Million Steps Along the Sea*.

This is Chindu's second work of fiction. His first novel, *I Who Killed My Brothers,* (available as *Epic Retold* in India), is also based on the Mahabharata, and available on Amazon.

I WHO KILLED MY BROTHERS

BHIMA'S STORY

Bhima is the second of the five Pandava princes, a mighty warrior who is never given his due by the world.

To everyone, including his own brothers, he is the 'blockhead', the 'idiot'. Even the delectable Draupadi, the queen the Pandavas share, treats Bhima with affectionate contempt.

But when their cousins cheat them out of their kingdom and enforce a thirteen-year exile, it is to the 'idiot' that everyone turns.

In this retelling of the Mahabharata, it is the 'idiot' — torn between his love for a forest woman and fierce loyalty to his brothers — who wins the crown for his family.

I who killed my brothers is the Mahabharata reinterpreted for the new generation. It tells the story of the feud between the Pandavas and the Kauravas — and the eighteen-day Kurukshetra War to end it.

Read the first chapters...

1

I STARE AT the lady with the black cloth over her eyes. I feel disturbed, scared – but I cannot look away.

Pale, beautiful face. Black strip wound tight. Beneath it, the eyes – the eyes with which she would not see.

Aunt Gandhari. The queen.

She hugs Mother, then us five. First, Yudhistira, then me, then Arjuna, then the twins, Nakula and Sahadeva. But why is she sobbing?

'Come,' Aunt Gandhari says. 'The king is waiting.'

She turns. I see the knot of blindfold, black against her grey hair. I stare.

I follow with Yudhistira, Mother and the younger ones. The palace doors close behind us.

So it is true? We are really princes?

We had all lived in the forest. Us five with Mother, Father, Ma Madri. The hermits there called our father 'King Pandu'. I had never understood that. I did not understand many things. Yudhistira said I was slow and stupid. But if Father was king, why were we living in a forest lodge?

I never got answers. Still, life was fun. Yudhistira sat with the hermits most of the time. Arjuna played with his bow and arrows. As for me, I wandered, hunting rabbits with my toy mace.

And I swam. Sometimes, when Yudhistira joined me, I would hold him underwater. Maybe I was slow and stupid, but I was strong. Very strong.

That day, Father had wandered off with Ma Madri, laughing. Mother sat by the window, still, silent. The next thing I remember was the wailing. I rushed out, Mother behind me. Ma Madri fell into her arms sobbing. Father had slipped, she said, hit his head on a rock. He was dead.

I ran along the forest path till I found where Father lay. There was blood on his face. I hadn't known him well; now I wouldn't.

That evening, they built a pyre. As the flames sprang up, I saw Ma Madri come out in her best robes. She hugged us each tight and walked to the pyre. Three times she circled it, head bent, lips moving. Then she turned, looked at us once – and walked into the flames. I wanted to look away, but I could not.

Ma Madri, she did not make a sound as the flames engulfed her.

Days later, men came in chariots. Mother spoke to them at length. After they left, she said, 'We are going to Hastinapur, our kingdom.'

And now we are walking through the palace – our palace? – with Aunt Gandhari. She walks alone, ahead, her blindfold black against her grey. I know the story of that blindfold. A balladeer sang about it on our last night in the forest, the first time she ever sang about our clan. Our aunt had vowed to cover her eyes and never see again when she learnt she was to wed Dritarashtra, the blind prince of Hastinapur.

Aunt Gandhari leads us to a doorway where two warriors cross spear points. They step aside. We walk into a huge hall lit by a hundred lamps, along a floor of polished marble. At the far end, on a golden throne, sits King Dritarashtra, our uncle.

He is huge – huge head, enormous chest, bulging arms – but not as huge as some of the foresters I have seen. Uncle is stronger than a thousand mad elephants, the balladeer had sung, the strongest man in the world. Is he? Really?

He rises. The sightless eyes stare straight at Mother. She says, 'I, Kunti, widow of your brother, bow before you.'

Uncle Dritarashtra places his hand on her head, then draws her into a long embrace. When he releases her, Yudhistira steps forward and prostrates. Then it is my turn. I hesitate. Someone pushes me forward. Uncle bends to touch my face, my shoulders, with hands that are surprisingly soft.

'Bhima has grown,' he says. 'Only five, but so tall! A warrior!'

His eyes are milky white, cold and dead. They devour me. 'I am glad you came,' he says finally, to Mother. 'Now I have five more sons.'

I know the king has many sons – a hundred, the songs said. Why aren't they here to greet us? I look around. And I see him.

He is my age, swathed in yellow silk robes. A gold necklace of many strands covers his chest. He stares at me fixedly from behind a pillar. I smile. He keeps staring. Then abruptly, he turns and walks away.

I stand there feeling foolish, angry with the boy, angrier with myself.

❋

I do not see him the next day. Or the next. But late one evening a week later, I come across him in one of the smaller courtyards. I am returning from another wander. Yudhistira has taken well to palace life – to the silk robes, the maids, the sleeping chambers. Not I.

I miss the forests, my old carefree life; I spend much of my time outdoors. This time, when I get back, the boy is standing in the shadows.

I have guessed who he is. Duryodhana, Uncle Dritarashtra's son, eldest of the Kaurava brothers. He steps forward.

I stop. I do not smile.

'So you are the one,' he says, 'the Pandava born to destroy my clan!'

That is one of the things I have heard the maids whisper. That, and that I was son of Vaayu, the God of Wind. I do not understand it. Nor do I understand why they say Yudhistira is the son of Yama Dharma, Arjuna the son of Indra. Was not Pandu our father? Now I hear it from the tongue of this haughty boy.

'Nothing to say, fat fool?' he taunts. 'They say you are stupid!'

I feel my anger rising. I step towards him.

'Aside!' I say.

The boy's eyes widen, the angry surprise of a palace prince unused to challenge. Then I see rage. I do not wait for him to attack. I push, my forehand against his gold-strung chest. I feel him resist, we strain for a split-second. He stumbles sideways.

Duryodhana is taller, bigger. But I am stronger – born to the forest, not to palace maids. I leave him against the wall.

I wait for Mother to chastise me the next day. She has not heard. Even the maids, who hear everything about everyone, have not heard. I am relieved – or am I? There is so much I want to ask Mother. Why do they say I am born to kill my own cousins? Why these tales about me?

The palace has changed our lives. Mother is rarely alone now and it is days before I get to speak to her in private. She frowns at my questions.

'Maids' tales!' she says, sitting me down. 'Do not pay heed. You are the son of Pandu and second in line to the throne of Hastinapur. Some day, your brother Yudhistira will be king. You have strength. It is your duty to support and protect him – always. It will not be easy... Pray to Vaayu, seek His blessings – be strong like the wind.'

That night, standing by my window, I close my eyes, I whisper: O Vaayu, God of Wind, bless me, protect me from harm, make me strong like you. And I feel the touch of a gentle breeze, soothing, wiping my fears away... my God is listening.

2

THE NEXT FEW weeks lend rhythm to my life.
Mornings, I wake up early to the sounds of conch and music from the palace courtyard. The maids would be waiting with hot water and fragrant oils for my bath. The bath fuels my hunger and, though forbidden to eat before school, I always stop to gulp down the meat dishes the maids smuggle me. Then it is time for Vedic school, for which I am inevitably late.

Grandfather Bhishma and Uncle Vidura, the most revered of our relatives, say our studies have suffered and we need to progress quickly. Grandfather has engaged a teacher, just for the five of us. Uncle Vidura's sons were to join us, but for some reason, they never do. Yudhistira is happy that they don't. Uncle Vidura, he says, is our father's half-brother, born to a maid, his sons not of royal lineage.

'They are sudhras, lower caste,' he tells me. 'They should not be allowed to sit with kshatriyas anyway.'

That is the thing about my elder brother. So very conscious about who is inferior to him, who his peer, what is right, what wrong. He loves the Vedic sessions. As for me, my favourite part of the day begins when we troop to Shukacharya to learn the crafts of war.

Our cousins are taught by Kripacharya. Grandfather Bhishma says we have a lot to learn before we can join them.

How good is Duryodhana then? I sometimes wonder.

Duryodhana pretends to ignore me, though at times, I see him watching me.

I love the sessions, but do not like the way everyone treats me. My teacher, my cousins, even my brothers, they all see me as fat, slow – and stupid. Kripacharya even says so when he gets angry. In his eyes, Yudhistira excels with chariots, Arjuna with the bow and arrow. Me? I am good only to wrestle or fight with the mace. Even there he sees Duryodhana as my better.

He is wrong. They all are. Or maybe, they just find it more amusing to laugh at the fat fool.

Let them laugh. Perhaps it is better they are blind to my strengths, blind to the hours of practice that I put in after lessons by myself.

I am growing strong, powerful. And more agile, fast on my feet, swift of arm and eye – swift like Vaayu, the God I pray to every night. In the chariot I am more fluid than Yudhistira. With the bow and arrow, though not blessed like Arjuna, I am more effective than others. Where I am more deliberate, Arjuna finds the target with no conscious effort. He says he'll be the greatest archer on earth. I believe him.

Arjuna believes the court singers' tale that Indra, king of all gods, is his father. He prays to him constantly.

If Arjuna is not with me, I usually slip into the elephant paddock after our mornings session. The mahouts indulge me; I am the only prince to visit them.

On one such occasion, as I finish grooming the little

tusker the mahouts have entrusted me with, I sense someone behind me. I turn around.

Duryodhana is watching me from the massive doorway, silent. He is not alone. With him are two others I recognize: Dushasana and Karna.

Dushasana is one of my cousins, a sad shadow of Duryodhana. Karna, I know of as the son of Athiratha, one of the palace charioteers. From afar, the son of the charioteer looks a bit like Yudhistira. But my brother would never have the scoff of scorn I see on Karna's face.

I do not want trouble. I step away from the elephant, moving quickly towards a side entrance. Footsteps rapidly close behind me. I stop.

'He is running away.' Duryodhana is laughing. 'The fat fool is afraid!'

Dushasana joins in.

'Look at him shake,' Karna says. 'Is this the one they say will destroy your clan, Duryodhana? This fat fool?'

Fat fool. I am used to that. But somehow, those words from Karna anger me more. What right does he have to call me that? I will pay him back – but not with words.

Knowing a confrontation is unavoidable, I turn around. Duryodhana has taken a fighting stance. I see Dushasana edging sideways. I take a deep breath.

I know what to expect. Duryodhana will lunge, try to grab me in a neck lock as we have been taught. Dushasana will attack my flank.

I pretend to watch Dushasana, turning slightly. As I see Duryodhana tensing, preparing to rush me, I pivot, kicking out hard at his knees.

Duryodhana falls heavily, yowling in pain. I turn quickly, allowing Dushasana to run into my elbow at the end of his clumsy offence. As he staggers, I shove him hard, sending him towards Duryodhana. He trips, falls over. I do not let them recover.

Slipping behind, I grab their hair. Their heads are slick with oil, but I get a good grip and tug hard. Their heads clash together. I repeat.

Again and again, I tug. They squirm, yell, but I do not stop. Karna has disappeared.

Shouts. Running feet. Rough hands wrench me away.

The mahouts surround Duryodhana and Dushasana. There is blood on Duryodhana's head and Dushasana's face. They are crying.

I slip away.

Much later, I approach Mother's chambers. Yudhistira is there. To my surprise, he embraces me. I return the hug, then touch Mother's feet.

'Son, why did you attack your cousins?' she asks quietly.

I didn't, I say. She looks at me for a long moment.

'That charioteer's son came to complain about you to Grandfather Bhishma,' Yudhistira says. 'He said you attacked them from behind.'

I tell them what really happened. They listen to me in silence.

'I understand why you fought,' Mother says finally, 'but did you have to hurt them so badly?'

I have no answer.

Mother pulls me close. 'Keep away from those boys, Bhima,' she says. 'They will try to harm you – and people will always blame you.'

I nod. Somehow that doesn't come as a surprise.

3

I STAY TRUE to my promise for months. It is only on the day I make my first kill – the day I become a true kshatriya – that I stray.

It is the royal tradition to hunt. A rite of passage for every prince, it is part of our education. Our father, I have heard courtiers say, loved hunting. Overindulged in it, in fact.

Being the younger brother, Father ought not have been king. But Grandfather Bhishma decided he would rule, for Uncle Dritarashtra was blind. Then one day, while away hunting, Father decided he would not return to the palace and that our uncle should rule instead. Why, I cannot fathom.

I am not thinking of that when we set out to the forest. Arjuna makes a fine kill, an arrow straight through the heart of a fleeing deer. Mine is considerably untidy and foolhardy. I somehow manage to spear a wild boar that charges me – more a case of dumb luck than skill.

It is late when we return. Perhaps it is the excitement of my first kill: for the first time in months, I walk to the river on my own. I want a moment of quiet to thank my God. I had felt him; he strengthened my arms when the boar charged.

Standing on the bank, I close my eyes. O, Vaayu, God of the Winds, bless your son, protect him the way you did today – always. And I feel him answer, a zephyr swirling in embrace, touching my face, whispering in my ears.

I strip, dive into the laughing Ganga. Down, down I go. I swim lazily back, and just as I am about to clamber on to the bank, I see him. He is not alone.

There is a crowd of them, Duryodhana at their head. Eager hands drag me out of the water. Fists rain on my back. I stumble and fall.

Rolling away, I gain my footing. The blows bother me but little. Fools, they are in each other's way; in their eagerness, they fail to hurt. As Duryodhana and Dushasana reach for me, I see my chance. Wrapping my arms around their necks, I take a deep breath and tumble back into the river.

I drag them down. Only when I feel their struggles grow weak do I let them break surface. They crawl on to the bank and fall, retching. I grab Duryodhana by his wet hair.

'Next time you attack me, I will kill you.

'And I will kill you,' I say, facing his crowd – the fools, the little boys, standing lost. 'All of you.'

I pick up my clothes and make for the palace, knowing well it has not ended.

I am summoned by Aunt Gandhari late that evening. Apprehensively, I walk to her chambers. Everyone is there, waiting. Aunt sits erect on the dais, Mother by her side. Duryodhana and his brothers stand to the left, in front, intently studying the floor. I walk to where Yudhistira, Arjuna and the twins wait.

'Have you already begun the war?' Aunt's voice is a whiplash in the silence.

She is addressing us all, but I feel her eyes boring into me through the blindfold. She continues, her voice trembling:

'The men of this palace have cared little for the tears of women. Women who have sacrificed so much – for blind and impotent men. If you have decided to follow that tradition, tell me now. I shall not wait to hear the sobs of the brides you bring here.'

Her voice softens. 'Child, Bhima, you are not born to destroy this clan. Duryodhana, your cousin, is not a wild animal to be hunted. But there are many here who tell you that. They teach you how to kill, but they do not teach you how to live like the brothers you are.'

She rises to her feet. 'If I hear you have been fighting again, I will leave this palace. Kill or die – that is your will.'

I see Duryodhana's stricken face as we turn to leave. I try to smile – and for the first time, I see my cousin beginning to respond.

The weeks that follow bring about a new balance in the palace. Aunt Gandhari's words have moved us all deeply. No longer do we avoid each other. We now speak and play together. Even the combat lessons are without much animosity.

By now the gurus have decided Duryodhana and I should focus on mace fighting. They appoint a teacher from afar for special lessons. The teacher is none other than our maternal cousin Balarama, of the Yadava clan, famed for his skills at mace warfare.

There is more technique to it than is evident from the outside. I work hard. Secretly, I also continue to practice with other weapons. Kripacharya may pretend I am skilled only with the mace, but I am determined to be more than a one-weapon warrior. A lot more.

Very often Duryodhana duels with me for practice. There is no ill will in the way we fight. As months pass, I begin to relax.

One afternoon, my cousin Chitrasena comes to find me. 'Aren't you going to the water pavilion in Pramanakoti?' he asks. 'Everyone is going.'

I hurriedly get ready. In the courtyard I see Duryodhana and the others waiting. Arjuna, Nakula and Sahadeva are there. But not Yudhistira. I find him in an inner room, engaged in his favourite pastime: a dice game. He gets up reluctantly.

We reach Pramanakoti in Duryodhana's chariot. 'Do not fear, Bhima,' he jokes, as we climb out. 'There'll be plenty of food when we finish!'

The others are already in the Ganga. I dive in. Some of the younger ones cling to me as I swim across and back. I continue swimming until Duryodhana shouts from the bank: 'Come on out, Bhima. Let us eat. I have a treat for you.'

Duryodhana has made arrangements in a secluded area. As I sit cross-legged in front of plates piled with food, he produces two mud pots.

'Soma,' he says. 'Drink fit for the gods!'

He takes a swig, pushing the second pot to me. I hesitate and then grab it with both hands. I do not want my cousin to know it is my first taste. I drink deep. The liquor burns my throat. I cough. Duryodhana laughs.

'My father is sending me to Dwaraka,' he says sometime

later, 'to continue learning mace warfare from Balarama. I will be invincible.'

Balarama is our mother's kin, yet it is Duryodhana who is going!

'I will be invincible too,' I blurt out. 'My father, Vaayu, will bless me!'

Duryodhana laughs loudly. 'Yudhistira, the son of Dharma. Bhima, the son of Vaayu. Arjuna, the son of Indra! Who believes all that? The impotent Pandu goes on a hunting expedition and suddenly he has sons. Five of them, all from Gods! How convenient!'

Karna is sniggering. Duryodhana continues, 'Paid singers tell the lie, palace maids retell it! You really are a fool to believe all that!'

I sit stunned, trying to absorb the crush of his words. He has called Mother immoral, us five illegitimate! With a roar, I jump to my feet.

Why are my knees so weak? Why am I collapsing? I try to stand, but my limbs do not obey. As I lie in the soft sand, I hear voices.

Shadowy figures encircle me. I feel them jostling. Then, in the crowd that peers down at me, I see Duryodhana's face. Holding on to Karna's shoulder, he is laughing.

4

I WAKE TO pain.

My chest feels like it is in a giant fist. I open my mouth to scream, only to swallow muddy river water. My hands are tied behind me, my ankles bound tight.

O Vaayu, is this the end of your son?

The sand is soft at the bottom. I kick hard towards the surface. Slowly, I begin to rise. Then a tug. The rope on my ankles has snared. A fury of panic engulfs me. Bending my knees, I kick out. My feet strike something solid, sharp. I repeat – again, again.

Suddenly, I am free. The rope on my ankles has loosened, allowing some movement. I begin to rise, lungs bursting. The surface is far, far away. As I feel the last of my breath burning out, my head bursts through. I gulp in a shuddering, sobbing breath.

I drift, rolling on to my back, using my feet to keep afloat. I do not know how far the current has carried me; it is a long time before I can think.

When I scan the horizon, I see land in the far distance. I begin to paddle, slowly, focusing only on holding my direction. It feels like hours. My legs are cramping and, just when I feel I will drown, my feet find sand. I can stand; the water is neck-deep here.

I half-wade, half-swim the rest of the way. It is hard to climb on to the bank with my arms tied. Dry ground again! I sob.

In the dark, I stumble on something and fall heavily. A sudden wave of dizziness overcomes me as I struggle to rise. I close my eyes.

It is light when I awaken. I am shivering. But it is not the cold that has disturbed me. A man crouches next, pressing a knife to my throat. He is small, wiry. Black hair falls past his shoulders. Eyes like the night search my face.

'Who are you?' he asks.

I give my name. He looks at me for a long time, then cuts me free. I try to rise, but sink back, no strength left in me.

'Who did this to you?' he asks, helping me sit up.

'Enemy,' I say. 'My brother.'

That does not seem to surprise him. 'Don't give him another chance,' he says. 'Kill him.'

As I look at him wordlessly, he disappears into the forest. A little later he returns. With him is another, a wizened but nimble old man. They have brought fruit. I learn about them as I eat. They are of the Naga tribe, the snake people, skilled hunters and bowmen.

When I finish, the old man hands me a bamboo hollow. It contains a green syrup that smells faintly of honey. I take a cautious sip. Juice of some herbs laced with honey. The old man motions me to finish it. Soon I begin to feel drowsy.

'Sleep now,' the younger Naga says.

The Nagas look after me well. On the seventh day, rested and energized, I bid goodbye to the people who had saved my life.

Everyone is surprised when I walk in through the Hastinapur gates. I am mud-stained, bare-chested, in deerskin. Ignoring the questions of the palace guards, I head straight for Mother's pavilion. Arjuna and Yudhistira are there when I enter.

Arjuna rushes to embrace me. Yudhistira stands by the window. I walk over to Mother and bend to touch her feet.

'Where were you?' Mother asks, holding me to her chest with a strength I never knew she possessed.

Motioning Arjuna to close the door, I sit down at her feet. Then, I tell them. Arjuna is the first to respond.

'Come, brother.' he says, jumping up. 'Let us teach Duryodhana a lesson he will never forget!'

'No. You will tell no one about this,' Mother says. 'Bhima, tomorrow you will rejoin your classes. Pretend nothing happened.'

Yudhistira makes as if to protest. Mother silences him with a look.

'There is nothing to be gained by accusing your cousins,' she says. 'All of you need to be careful from now on, particularly Bhima.'

I learn that my cousins had said I drank soma, then wandered off. 'Duryodhana even joined us when we went looking for you,' Arjuna says.

I nod. It is as I expected. We pay our respects to Mother and walk to our rooms. Her voice follows me: 'Be careful. Very careful.'

The surprise over my return does not last long. I tell all who ask part-truth: I fell into the river, was carried downstream, then got lost. No one questions me closely, mainly because a new martial arts guru has the palace's rapt attention.

The famed Dronacharya is not of the warrior caste, but a brahmin. Word of his arrival has spread; there are many new faces at our lessons. But missing is a face I have been searching for: Karna's. I learn Dronacharya has refused to teach him, citing his low birth.

It soon becomes clear to me Dronacharya is partial, even more than Kripacharya. He has definite ideas on what each student should do.

'The mace is your weapon, Bhima,' he tells me, seeing me practice chariot warfare. 'Leave chariots and archery to others more capable.'

I nod with a respect I don't feel. Inwardly, I vow to practice even harder, determined more than ever to master all forms of combat.

Arjuna is clearly Dronacharya's favourite. My brother plays up to him unashamedly, spending hours practising archery as the master looks on. Yet Arjuna is not satisfied. He feels the master is holding back, saving his secret techniques for his own son, Ashwathama.

'It is not fair,' Arjuna complains. I smile. Though it is Ashwathama my brother speaks of often, I know he is worrying about Karna.

'I wonder how Karna is faring,' I say, just to tease Arjuna. 'I hear he has found a new teacher – someone who is teaching him everything!'

Arjuna scowls. 'I am better than him, brother,' he says. 'You will see on exhibition day!'

I am also looking forward to the day when we demonstrate our skills before a select audience. I might well get my chance then. Since my return, I have been waiting to get Duryodhana alone, but to no avail. At the exhibition, though, he might be pitted against me.

I do not see Arjuna much in the following weeks. I suppose he is busy, training hard.

One of mahouts, meanwhile, has found me a charioteer, who helps with my training. His name is Visoka. Only five years older than me, he is a master with the reins. Every evening, Visoka and I head out to practise chariot drills. I soon realize Visoka is no regular charioteer. He is a brilliant strategist, adept at all warcraft, and I grow to trust him more and more.

On the morning of the exhibition day, he is waiting for me. We drive slowly towards the arena. The galleries are already full. In the royal enclosure I see Uncle Dritarashtra and Aunt Gandhari. Sanjaya, who serves as Uncle's eyes, stands behind. Mother is there too.

Standing in the middle of the arena, Dronacharya begins to call out names after the rituals are over. The competition has begun.

In no mood to watch, I climb on to the chariot and wait. After a long time, in a silence punctuating the roar of the crowd, I hear my name.

I who killed my brothers is available on Amazon. Buy now!

DEAR READER

Thank you for reading this book. I hope you enjoyed this version of the Mahabharata. Please do leave a review, either at the online bookstall or on Goodreads!

CS

www.epicretold.co.uk
@epicretold
@chindu
www.chindu.co.uk